NO SCHOOL TODAY!

By Franz Brandenberg
Illustrated by Aliki

SCHOLASTIC INC.
New York Toronto London Auckland Sydney

ISBN 0-590-11888-9

Text copyright © 1975 by Franz Brandenberg.
Illustrations copyright © 1975 by Aliki Brandenberg.
This edition is published by Scholastic Inc., by arrangement with
Macmillan Publishing Co., Inc.

19 18 17 16 15 14 13 12 11 10 9 8   5 6 7 8 9/8 0/9

Printed in the U.S.A.   07

To Susan C. Hirschman

Edward and Elizabeth finished their breakfast
at a quarter to eight.

At five to eight their teeth were brushed.

At eight o'clock they stood at the door.

"For a change you are early," said their mother.

"You don't have to rush," said their father.

"We are early," said Edward.

"School won't start for another hour."

"For a change we have lots of time," said Elizabeth.

They watched workers build a house.

They watched firemen put out a fire.

They looked at a bakery window.

They studied a pet shop window.

And they stood a long time in front of
the toy store window.

"Let's go to school!" said Elizabeth.

"It must be late."

They ran all the way to school.

The halls were empty.

"We are late," said Elizabeth.

The classrooms were empty.

"There is no school today," said Edward.

"Let's go home!"

"No school today!" they shouted at
the children coming up the steps.

"No school today!" they shouted at
the children coming down the street.

"No school today!" they shouted to the teacher.

"No school today!" they called to the principal.

"What happened?" asked their father.

"Why are you back?" asked their mother.

"No school today!" said Edward and Elizabeth.

"Who told you?" asked their mother.

"No one," said Edward.

"There's no one at school," said Elizabeth.

"It is only five to nine," said their father.

"I told you, you were early," said their mother.

"I told you, you didn't have to rush," said their father.

"If we don't rush now, we will be late," said Elizabeth.

They ran all the way to school,

and got there just on time.

The end